SIMON AND SCHUSTER

First published in Great Britain
in 2015 by Simon and Schuster
UK Ltd · 1st Floor, 222 Gray's
Inn Road, London WC1X 8HB
A CBS Company · Text
copyright © 2015 Caryl Hart
Illustrations   copyright
© 2015 Deborah Allwright
The right of Caryl Hart and
Deborah Allwright to be
identified as the author and
illustrator of this work has
been asserted by them in
accordance with the Copyright,
Designs and Patents Act, 1988
All rights reserved, including
the right of reproduction in
whole or in part in any form
A CIP catalogue record for
this book is available from the
British Library upon request
ISBN: 978-0-85707-612-0 HB
ISBN: 978-0-85707-613-7 PB
Printed in China
10 9 8 7 6 5 4 3 2 1

FOR IMMA & MATHILDE -
YOU ARE AMAZING! - C.H.

FOR KAI & POPPY
LOVE D.A.

Visit www.carylhart.com and www.deborahallwright.com

The inclusion of author or illustrator website addresses in this book does not constitute
an endorsement by or an association with Simon and Schuster UK Ltd of such sites or the
content, products, advertising or other materials presented on such sites.

there's a MONSTER in my fridge

KEEP OUT!

CARYL HART

Deborah Allwright

SIMON AND SCHUSTER
London   New York   Sydney   Toronto   New Delhi

What's that hiding behind the door?
Its feet have **squelched** across the floor . . .

Take care! Don't look! It's vile and smelly.

A MONSTER

eating raspberry jelly!

What's that hiding behind the screen,
With a **pointy hat** and **skin so green**?

A WITCH

is using glitter glue!

Below our stairs, it's **dark** and **cold**.

It's full of **spiders**, dust and mould.

A VAMPIRE

in his underwear!

What's that **splashing** in our bath?
It has a hollow, **rattly** laugh.

Tucked in bed, there's something **scary**.
Its fangs are **sharp**, its back is

HAIRY!

Lift the sheet. What will you find?

But look, what's this? A secret door!
A staircase to another floor.

Quiet as mice, don't dare to speak.
Slowly, lift the trap door . . .

CREAK!

Tiptoe carefully as can be, who's that hiding?

BOO!

It's me!

A WEREWOLF

scratching his behind!